The King's Betrothed
(A Story Sketched from Life.)

By

E. T. A. Hoffmann

British Library Cataloguing-in-Publication Data
A catalogue record for this book is available from the
British Library

Contents

E. T. A. Hoffman

Ernst Theodor Wilhelm Hoffmann was born in Königsberg, East Prussia in 1776. His family were all jurists, and during his youth he was initially encouraged to pursue a career in law. However, in his late teens Hoffman became increasingly interested in literature and philosophy, and spent much of his time reading German classicists and attending lectures by, amongst others, Immanuel Kant.

In was in his twenties, upon moving with his uncle to Berlin, that Hoffman first began to promote himself as a composer, writing an operetta called Die Maske and entering a number of playwriting competitions. Hoffman struggled to establish himself anywhere for a while, flitting between a number of cities and dodging the attentions of Napoleon's occupying troops. In 1808, while living in Bamberg, he began his job as a theatre manager and a music critic, and Hoffman's break came a year later, with the publication of Ritter Gluck. The story centred on a man who meets, or thinks he has met, a long-dead composer, and played into the 'doppelgänger' theme – at that time very popular in literature. It was shortly after this that Hoffman began to use the pseudonym E. T. A. Hoffmann, declaring the 'A' to stand for 'Amadeus', as a tribute to the great composer, Mozart.

Over the next decade, while moving between Dresden, Leipzig and Berlin, Hoffman produced a great range of both literary and musical works. Probably Hoffman's most well-known story, produced in 1816, is 'The Nutcracker and the Mouse King', due to the fact that – some seventy-six years later - it inspired Tchaikovsky's ballet The Nutcracker.

In the same vein, his story 'The Sandman' provided both the inspiration for Léo Delibes's ballet Coppélia, and the basis for a highly influential essay by Sigmund Freud, called 'The Uncanny'. (Indeed, Freud referred to Hoffman as the "unrivalled master of the uncanny in literature.")

Alcohol abuse and syphilis eventually took a great toll on Hoffman though, and – having spent the last year of his life paralysed – he died in Berlin in 1822, aged just 46. His legacy is a powerful one, however: He is seen as a pioneer of both Romanticism and fantasy literature, and his novella, Mademoiselle de Scudéri: A Tale from the Times of Louis XIV is often cited as the first ever detective story.

Chapter I.

Which Gives An Account Of The Various Characters, And Their Mutual Relations To Each Other, And Prepares The Way, Pleasantly, For The Many Marvellous And Most Entertaining Matters Of Which The Succeeding Chapters Treat.

It was a blessed year. In the fields the corn, the wheat, and the barley grew most gloriously. The boys waded in the grass, and the cattle in the clover. The trees hung so full of cherries that, with the best will in the world, the great army of the sparrows, though determined to peck everything bare, were forced to leave half the fruit for a future feast. Every creature filled itself full every day at the great guest-table of nature. Above all, however, the vegetables in Herr Dapsul von Zabelthau's kitchen-garden had turned out such a splendid and beautiful crop that it was no wonder Fräulein Aennchen was unable to contain herself with joy on the subject.

We may here explain who Herr Dapsul von Zabelthau and Aennchen were.

Perhaps, dear reader, you may have at some time found yourself in that beautiful country which is watered by the pleasant, kindly river Main. Soft morning breezes, breathing their perfumed breath over the plain as it shimmered in the golden splendour of the new-risen sun, you found it impossible to sit cooped up in your stuffy carriage, and you alighted and wandered into the little grove, through the trees of which, as you descended towards the valley, you came in sight of a little village. And as you were gazing, there would suddenly come towards you, through the trees, a tall, lanky man, whose strange dress and appearance riveted your attention. He had on a small grey felt hat on the top of a black periwig: all his clothes were grey--coat, vest, and breeches, grey stockings-- even his walking-stick coloured grey. He would come up to you with long strides, and staring at you with great sunken eyes, seemingly not aware of your existence, would cry out, almost running you down, "Good morning, sir!" And then, like one awaking from a dream, he would add in a hollow, mournful voice, "Good morning! Oh, sir, how thankful we ought to be that we have a good, fine morning. The poor people at Santa Cruz just had two earthquakes, and now- -at this moment--rain falling in torrents." While you have been thinking what to say to this strange creature, he, with an "Allow me, sir," has gently passed his hand across your brow, and inspected the palm of your hand. And saying, in the same hollow, melancholy accents as before, "God bless you, sir! You have a good constellation," has gone striding on his way.

This odd personage was none other than Herr Dapsul Von Zabelthau, whose sole--rather miserable--possession is the village, or hamlet, of Dapsulheim, which lies before you in this most pleasant and smiling country into which you now enter. You are looking forward to something in the shape of breakfast, but in the little inn things have rather a gloomy aspect. Its small store of provisions was cleared out at the fair, and as you can't be expected to be content with nothing besides milk, they tell you to go to the Manor House, where the gracious Fräulein Anna will entertain you hospitably with whatever may be forthcoming there. Accordingly, thither you betake yourself without further ceremony.

Concerning this Manor House, there is nothing further to say than that it has doors and windows, as of yore had that of Baron Tondertontonk in Westphalia. But above the hall-door the family coat-of-arms makes a fine show, carved there in wood with New Zealand skilfulness. And this Manor House derives a peculiar character of its own from the circumstance that its north side leans upon the enceinte, or outer line of defence belonging to an old ruined castle, so that the back entrance is what was formerly the castle gate, and through it one passes at once into the courtyard of that castle, in the middle of which the tall watch-tower still stands undamaged. From the hall door, which is surmounted by the coat-of-arms, there comes meeting you a red-cheeked young lady, who, with her clear blue eyes and fair hair, is to be called very pretty indeed, although her figure may be considered just the least bit too roundly substantial. A personification of friendly kindness, she begs you to go in, and as soon as she ascertains your wants, serves you up the most delicious milk, a liberal allowance of first-rate bread and butter, uncooked ham--as good as you would find in Bayonne--and a small glass of beetroot brandy. Meanwhile, this young lady (who is none other than Fräulein Anna von Zabelthau) talks to you gaily and pleasantly of rural matters, displaying anything but a limited knowledge of such subjects. Suddenly, however, there resounds a loud and terrible voice, as if from the skies, crying "Anna, Anna, Anna!" This rather startles you; but Fräulein Anna says, pleasantly, "There's papa back from his walk, calling for his breakfast from his study." "Calling from his study," you repeat, or enquire, astonished. "Yes," says Fräulein Anna, or Fräulein Aennchen, as the people call her. "Yes; papa's study is up in the tower there, and he calls down through the speaking trumpet." And you see Aennchen open the narrow door of the old lower, with a similar déjeuner à la fourchette to that which you have had yourself, namely, a liberal helping of bread and ham, not forgetting the beetroot brandy, and go briskly in at it. But she is back directly, and taking you all over the charming kitchen-garden, has so much to say about feather-sage, rapuntika, English turnips, little greenheads, montrue, great yellow, and so forth, that you have no idea that all these fine names merely mean various descriptions of cabbages and salads.

I think, dear reader, that this little glimpse which you have had of Dapsulheim is sufficient to enable you to understand all the outs and ins of the establishment, concerning which I have to narrate to you all manner of extraordinary, barely comprehensible, matters and occurrences. Herr Dapsul von Zabelthau had, during his youth, very rarely left his parents' country place. They had been people of considerable means. His tutor, after teaching him foreign languages, particularly those of the East, fostered a natural inclination which he possessed towards mysticism, or rather, occupying himself with the mysterious. This tutor died, leaving as a legacy to young Dapsul a whole library of occult science, into the very depths of which he proceeded to plunge. His parents dying, he betook himself to long journeyings, and (as his tutor had impressed him with the necessity of doing) to Egypt and India. When he got home again, after many years, a cousin had looked after his affairs with such zeal that there was nothing left to him but the little hamlet of Dapsulheim. Herr Dapsul was too eagerly occupied in the pursuit of the sun-born gold of a higher sphere to trouble himself about that which was earthly. He rather felt obliged to his cousin for preserving to him the pleasant, friendly Dapsulheim, with the fine, tall tower, which might have been built expressly on purpose for astrological operations, and in the upper storey and topmost height of which he at once established his study. And indeed he thanked his said cousin from the bottom of his heart.

This careful cousin now pointed out that Herr Dapsul von Zabelthau was bound to marry. Dapsul immediately admitted the necessity, and, without more ado, married at once the lady whom his cousin had selected for him. This lady disappeared almost as quickly as she had appeared on the scene. She died, after bearing him a daughter. The cousin attended to the marriage, the baptism, and the funeral; so that Dapsul, up in his tower, paid very little attention to either. For there was a very remarkable comet visible during most of the time, and Dapsul, ever melancholy and anticipative of evil, considered that he was involved in its influence.

The little daughter, under the careful up-bringing of an

old grand-aunt, developed a remarkable aptitude for rural affairs. She had to begin at the very beginning, and, so to speak, rise from the ranks, serving successively as goose-girl, maid-of-all-work, upper farm-maid, housekeeper, and, finally, as mistress, so that Theory was all along illustrated and impressed upon her mind by a salutary share of Practice. She was exceedingly fond of ducks and geese, hens and pigeons, and even the tender broods of well-shaped piglings she was by no means indifferent to, though she did not put a ribbon and a bell round a little white sucking-pig's neck and make it into a sort of lap-dog, as a certain young lady, in another place, was once known to do. But more than anything--more than even to the fruit trees--she was devoted to the kitchen-garden. From her grand-aunt's attainments in this line she had derived very remarkable theoretical knowledge of vegetable culture (which the reader has seen for himself), as regarded digging of the ground, sowing the seed, and setting the plants. Fräulein Aennchen not only superintended all these operations, but lent most valuable manual aid. She wielded a most vigorous spade--her bitterest enemy would have admitted this. So that while Herr Dapsul von Zabelthau was immersed in astrological observations and other important matters, Fräulein Aennchen carried on the management of the place in the ablest possible manner, Dapsul looking after the celestial part of the business, and Aennchen managing the terrestrial side of things with unceasing vigilance and care.

As above said, it was small wonder that Aennchen was

almost beside herself with delight at the magnificence of the yield which this season had produced in the kitchen-garden. But the carrot-bed was what surpassed everything else in the garden in its promise.

"Oh, my dear, beautiful carrots!" cried Anna over and over again, and she clapped her hands, danced, and jumped about, and conducted herself like a child who has been given a grand Christmas present.

And indeed it seemed as though the carrot-children underground were taking part in Aennchen's gladness, for some extremely delicate laughter, which just made itself heard, was undoubtedly proceeding from the carrot-bed. Aennchen didn't, however, pay much heed to it, but ran to meet one of the farm-men who was coming, holding up a letter, and calling out to her, "For you, Fräulein Aennchen. Gottlieb brought it from the town."

Aennchen saw immediately, from the hand writing, that it was from none other than young Herr Amandus von Nebelstern, the son of a neighbouring proprietor, now at the university. During the time when he was living at home, and in the habit of running over to Dapsulheim every day, Amandus had arrived at the conviction that in all his life he never could love anybody except Aennchen. Similarly, Aennchen was perfectly certain that she could never really care the least bit about anybody else but this brown-locked Amandus. Thus both Aennchen and Amandus had come to the conclusion and arrangement that they were to be married as soon as ever they could--the sooner the better--and be the very happiest married couple in the wide world.

Amandus had at one time been a bright, natural sort of lad enough, but at the university he had got into the hands of God knows who, and had been induced to fancy himself a marvellous poetical genius, as also to betake himself to an extreme amount of absurd extravagance in expression of ideas. He carried this so far that he soon soared far away beyond everything which prosaic idiots term Sense and Reason (maintaining at the same time, as they do, that both are perfectly co-existent with the utmost liveliness of imagination).

It was from this young Amandus that the letter came which Aennchen opened and read, as follows:--

"HEAVENLY MAIDEN,--

"Dost thou see, dost thou feel, dost thou not image and figure to thyself, thy Amandus, how, circumambiated by the orange-flower-laden breath of the dewy evening, he is lying on his back in the grass, gazing heavenward with eyes filled with the holiest love and the most longing adoration? The thyme and the lavender, the rose and the gilliflower, as also the yellow-eyed narcissus and the shamefaced violet--he weaveth into garlands. And the flowers are love-thoughts--thoughts of thee, oh, Anna! But doth feeble prose beseem inspired lips? Listen! oh, listen how I can only love, and speak of my love, sonnetically!

"Love flames aloft in thousand eager sunspheres,

Joy wooeth joy within the heart so warmly:

Down from the darkling sky soft stars are shining.

Back-mirrored from the deep, still wells of love-tears.
"Delight, alas! doth die of joy too burning--
The sweetest fruit hath aye the bitt'rest kernel--
While longing beckons from the violet distance,
In pain of love my heart to dust is turning.
"In fiery billows rage the ocean surges,
Yet the bold swimmer dares the plunge full arduous,
And soon amid the waves his strong course urges.
"And on the shore, now near, the jacinth shoots:
The faithful heart holds firm: 'twill bleed to death;
But heart's blood is the sweetest of all roots.[1]

"Oh, Anna! when thou readest this sonnet of all sonnets, may all the heavenly rapture permeate thee in which all my being was dissolved when I wrote it down, and then read it out, to kindred minds, conscious, like myself, of life's highest. Think, oh, think I sweet maiden of

"Thy faithful, enraptured,

"AMANDUS VON NEBELSTERN.

"P.S.--Don't forget, oh, sublime virgin! when answering this, to send a pound or two of that Virginia tobacco which you grow yourself. It burns splendidly, and has a far better flavour than the Porto Rico which the Bürschen smoke when they go to the Kneipe."

[Footnote 1: The translator may point out that the original of this nonsense is, itself, intentionally nonsense, and that he has done his best to render it into English--not an easy task.--A. E.]

Fräulein Aennchen pressed the letter to her lips, and said, "Oh, how dear, how beautiful! And the darling verses, rhyming so beautifully. Oh, if I were only clever enough to understand it all; but I suppose nobody can do that but a student. I wonder what that about the 'roots' means? I suppose it must be the long red English carrots, or, who knows, it may be the rapuntica. Dear fellow!"

That very day Fräulein Aennchen made it her business to pack up the tobacco, and she took a dozen of her finest goose-quills to the schoolmaster, to get him to make them into pens. Her intention was to sit down at once and begin her answer to the precious letter. As she was going out of the kitchen-garden, she was again followed by a very faint, almost imperceptible, sound of delicate laughter; and if she had paid a little attention to what was going on, she would have been sure to hear a little delicate voice saying, "Pull me, pull me! I am ripe--ripe--ripe!" However, as we have said, she paid no attention, and did not hear this.

CHAPTER II.

WHICH CONTAINS AN ACCOUNT OF THE FIRST WONDERFUL EVENT, AND OTHER MATTERS DESERVING OF PERUSAL, WITHOUT WHICH THIS TALE COULD HAVE HAD NO EXISTENCE.

Herr Dapsul Von Zabelthau generally came down from his astronomical tower about noon, to partake of a frugal repast with his daughter, which usually lasted a very short time, and during which there was generally a great predominance of silence, for Dapsul did not like to talk. And Aennchen did not trouble him by speaking much, and this all the more for the reason that if her papa did actually begin to talk, he would come out with all sorts of curious unintelligible nonsense, which made a body's head giddy. This day, however, her head was so full, and her mind so excited and taken up with the flourishing state of the kitchen-garden, and the letter from her beloved Amandus, that she talked of both subjects incessantly, mixed up, without leaving off. At last Herr Dapsul von Zabelthau laid down his knife and fork, stopped his ears with his hands, and cried out, "Oh, the dreary higgledy-piggledy of chatter and gabble!"

Aennchen stopped, alarmed, and he went on to say, in the melancholy sustained tones which were characteristic of him, "With regard to the vegetables, my dear daughter, I have long been cognizant that the manner in which the stars have worked together this season has been eminently favourable to those growths, and the earthly man will be amply supplied with cabbage, radishes, and lettuce, so that the earthly matter may duly increase and withstand the fire of the world-spirit, like a properly kneaded pot. The gnomic principle will resist the attacks of the salamander, and I shall have the enjoyment of eating the parsnips which you cook so well. With regard to young Amandus von Nebelstern, I have not the slightest objection to your marrying him as soon as he comes back from the university. Simply send Gottlieb up to tell me when your marriage is going to take place, so that I may go with you to the church."

Herr Dapsul kept silence for a few seconds, and then, without looking at Aennchen, whose face was glowing with delight, he went on, smiling and striking his glass with his fork (two things which he seldom did at all, though he always did them together) to say, "Your Amandus has got to be, and cannot help being, where and what he is. He is, in fact, a gerund; and I shall merely tell you, my dear Aennchen, that I drew up his horoscope a long while ago. His constellation is favourable enough on the whole, for the matter of that. He has Jupiter in the ascending node, Venus regarding in the sextile. The trouble is, that the path of Sirius cuts across, and, just at the point of intersection, there is a great danger from which Amandus delivers his betrothed. The danger--what it is--is indiscoverable, because some strange being, which appears to set at defiance all astrological science, seems to be concerned in it. At the same time, it is evident and certain

18

that it is only the strange psychical condition which mankind terms craziness, or mental derangement, which will enable Amandus to accomplish this deliverance. Oh, my daughter!" (here Herr Dapsul fell again into his usual pathetic tone), "may no mysterious power, which keeps itself hidden from my seer-eyes, come suddenly across your path, so that young Amandus von Nebelstern may not have to rescue you from any other danger but that of being an old maid." He sighed several times consecutively, and then continued, "But the path of Sirius breaks off abruptly after this danger, and Venus and Jupiter, divided before, come together again, reconciled."

Herr Dapsul von Zabelthau had not spoken so much for years as on this occasion. He arose exhausted, and went back up into his tower.

Aennchen had her answer to Herr von Nebelstern ready in good time next morning. It was as follows:--

"My own dearest Amandus--

"You cannot believe what joy your letter has given me. I have told papa about it, and he has promised to go to church with us when we're married. Be sure to come back from the university as soon as ever you can. Oh! if I only could quite understand your darling verses, which rhyme so beautifully. When I read them to myself aloud they sound wonderful, and then I think I do understand them quite well. But soon everything grows confused, and seems to get away from me, and I feel as if I had been reading a lot of mere words that somehow don't belong to each other at all. The schoolmaster says this must be so, and that it's the new fashionable way of speaking. But, you see, I'm--oh, well!--I'm only a stupid, foolish creature. Please to write and tell me if I couldn't be a student for a little time, without neglecting my housework. I suppose that couldn't be, though, could it? Well, well: when once we're husband and wife, perhaps I may pick up a little of your learning, and learn a little of this new, fashionable way of speaking.

"I send you the Virginian tobacco, my dearest Amandus. I've packed my bonnet-box full of it, as much as ever I could get into it; and, in the meantime, I've put my new straw hat on to Charles the Great's head--you know he stands in the spare bedroom, although he has no feet, being only a bust, as you remember.

"Please don't laugh, Amandus dear; but I have made some poetry myself, and it rhymes quite nicely, some of it. Write and tell me how a person, without learning, can know so well what rhymes to what? Just listen, now--

"I love you, dearest, as my life.

And long at once to be your wife.

The bright blue sky is full of light,

When evening comes the stars shine bright.

So you must love me always truly,

And never cause me pain unduly,

I pack up the 'baccy you asked me to send,

And I hope it will yield you enjoyment no end.

"There! you must take the will for the deed, and when I learn the fashionable way of speaking, I'll do some better poetry. The yellow lettuces are promising splendidly this year--never was such a crop; so are the French beans; but my little dachshund, Feldmann, gave the big gander a terrible bite in the leg yesterday. However, we can't have everything perfect in this world. A hundred kisses in imagination, my dearest Amandus, from

"Your most faithful fiancée,

"Anna von Zabelthau.

"P.S.--I've been writing in an awful hurry, and that's the reason the letters are rather crooked here and there.

"P.S.--But you mustn't mind about that. Though I may write a little crookedly, my heart is all straight, and I am

"Always your faithful

"Anna.

"P.S.--Oh, good gracious! I had almost forgot-- thoughtless thing that I am. Papa sends you his kind regards, and says you have got to be, and cannot help being, where and what you are; and that you are to rescue me from a terrible danger some day. Now, I'm very glad of this, and remain, once more,

"Your most true and loving

"Anna von Zabelthau."

It was a good weight off Fräulein Aennchen's mind when she had written this letter; it had cost her a considerable effort. So she felt light-hearted and happy when she had put it in its envelope, sealed it up without burning the paper or her own fingers, and given it, together with the bonnet-boxful of tobacco, to Gottlieb to take to the post-office in the town. When she had seen properly to the poultry in the yard, she ran as fast as she could to the place she loved best--the kitchen-garden. When she got to the carrot-bed she thought it was about time to be thinking of the sweet-toothed people in the town, and be palling the earliest of the carrots. The servant-girl was called in to help in this process. Fräulein Aennchen walked, gravely and seriously, into the middle of the bed, and grasped a stately carrot-plant. But on her pulling at it a strange sound made itself heard. Do not, reader, think of the witches' mandrake-root, and the horrible whining and howling which pierces the heart of man when it is drawn from the earth. No; the tone which was heard on this occasion was like very delicate, joyous laughter. But Fräulein Aennchen let the carrot-plant go, and cried out, rather frightened, "Eh! Who's that laughing at me?" But there being nothing more to be heard she took hold of the carrot-plant again--which seemed to be finer and better grown than any of the rest--and, notwithstanding the laughing, which began again, pulled up the very finest and most splendid carrot ever beheld by mortal eye. When she looked at it more closely she gave a cry of joyful surprise, so that the maid-servant came running up; and she also exclaimed aloud at the beautiful miracle which disclosed itself to her eyes. For there was a beautiful ring firmly attached to the carrot, with a shining topaz mounted in it.

"Oh," cried the maid, "that's for you! It's your wedding-ring. Put it on directly."

"Stupid nonsense!" said Fräulein Aennchen. "I must get my wedding-ring from Herr Amandus von Nebelstern, not from a carrot."

However, the longer she looked at the ring the better she was pleased with it; and, indeed, it was of such wonderfully fine workmanship that it seemed to surpass anything ever produced by human skill. On the ring part of it there were hundreds and hundreds of tiny little figures twined together in the most manifold groupings, hardly to be made out with the naked eye at first, so microscopically minute were they. But when one looked at them closely for a little while they appeared to grow bigger and more distinct, and to come to life, and dance in pretty combinations. And the fire of the gem was of such a remarkable water that the like of it could not have been found in the celebrated Dresden collection.

"Who knows," said the maid, "how long this beautiful ring may have been underground? And it must have got shoved up somehow, and then the carrot has grown right through it."

Fräulein Aennchen took the ring off the carrot, and it was strange how the latter suddenly slipped through her fingers and disappeared in the ground. But neither she nor the maid paid much heed to this circumstance, being lost in admiration of the beautiful ring, which the young lady immediately put on the little finger of the right hand without more ado. As she did so, she felt a stinging pain all up her finger, from the root of it to the point; but this pain went away again as quickly as it had come.

Of course she told her father, at mid-day, all about this strange adventure at the carrot-bed, and showed him the beautiful ring which had been sticking upon the carrot. She was going to take it off that he might examine it the better, but felt the same stinging kind of pain as when she put it on. And this pain lasted all the time she was trying to get it off, so that she had to give up trying. Herr Dapsul scanned the ring upon her finger with the most careful attention. He made her stretch her finger out, and describe with it all sorts of circles in all directions. After which he fell into a profound meditation, and went up into his tower without uttering a syllable. Aennchen heard him giving vent to a very considerable amount of groaning and sighing as he went.

Next morning, when she was chasing the big cock about the yard (he was bent on all manner of mischief, and was skirmishing particularly with the pigeons), Herr Dapsul began lamenting so fearfully down from the tower through the speaking trumpet that she cried up to him through her closed hand, "Oh papa dear, what are you making such a terrible howling for? The fowls are all going out of their wits."

Heir Dapsul hailed down to her through the speaking trumpet, saying, "Anna, my daughter Anna, come up here to me immediately."

Fräulein Aennchen was much astonished at this command, for her papa had never in all his life asked her to go into the tower, but rather had kept the door of it carefully shut. So that she was conscious of a certain sense of anxiety as she climbed the narrow winding stair, and opened the heavy door which led into its one room. Herr Dapsul von Zabelthau was seated upon a large armchair of singular form, surrounded by curious instruments and dusty books. Before him was a kind of stand, upon which there was a paper stretched in a frame, with a number of lines drawn upon it. He had on a tall pointed cap, a wide mantle of grey calimanco, and on his chin a long white beard, so that he had quite the appearance of a magician. On account of his false beard, Aennchen didn't know him a bit just at first, and looked curiously about to see if her father were hidden away in some corner; but when she saw that the man with the beard on was really papa, she laughed most heartily, and asked if it was Yule-time, and he was going to act Father Christmas.

Paying no heed to this enquiry, Herr Dapsul von Zabelthau took a small tool of iron in his hand, touched Aennchen's forehead with it, and then stroked it along her right arm several times, from the armpit to the tip of the little finger. While this was going on she had to sit in the armchair, which he had quitted, and to lay the finger which had the ring upon it on the paper which was in the frame, in such a position that the topaz touched the central point where all the lines came together. Yellow rays immediately shot out from the topaz all round, colouring the paper all over with deep yellow light. Then the lines went flickering and crackling up and down, and the little figures which were on the ring seemed to be jumping merrily about all over the paper. Herr Dapsul, without taking his eyes from the paper, had taken hold of a thin plate of some metal, which he held up high over his head with both arms, and was proceeding to press it down upon the paper; but ere he could do so he slipped his foot on the smooth stone floor, and fell, anything but softly, upon the sitting portion of his body; whilst the metal plate, which he had dropped in an instinctive attempt to break his fall, and save damage to his Os Coccygis, went clattering down upon the stones. Fräulein Aennchen awoke, with a gentle "Ah!" from a strange dreamy condition in which she had been. Herr Dapsul with some difficulty raised himself, put the grey sugar-loaf cap, which had fallen off, on again, arranged the false beard, and sate himself down opposite to Aennchen upon a pile of folio volumes.

"My daughter," he said, "my daughter Anna; what were your sensations? Describe your thoughts, your feelings? What were the forms seen by the eye of the spirit within your inner being?"

"Ah!" answered Anna, "I was so happy; I never was so happy in all my life. And I thought of Amandus von Nebelstern. And I saw him quite plainly before my eyes, but he was much better looking than he used to be, and he was smoking a pipe of the Virginian tobacco that I sent him, and seemed to be enjoying it tremendously. Then all at once I felt a great appetite for young carrots with sausages; and lo and behold! there the dishes were before me, and I was just going to help myself to some when I woke up from the dream in a moment, with a sort of painful start."

"Amandus von Nebelstern, Virginia canaster, carrots, sausages," quoth Herr Dapsul von Zabelthau to his daughter very reflectively. And he signed to her to stay where she was, for she was preparing to go away.

"Happy is it for you, innocent child," he began, in a tone much more lamentable than even his usual one, "that you are as yet not initiated into the profounder mysteries of the universe, and are unaware of the threatening perils which surround you. You know nothing of the supernatural science of the sacred cabbala. True, you will never partake the celestial joy of those wise ones who, having attained the highest step, need never eat or drink except for their pleasure, and are exempt from human necessities. But then, you have not to endure and suffer the pain of attainment to that step, like your unhappy father, who is still far more liable to attacks of mere human giddiness, to whom that which he laboriously discovers only causes terror and awe, and who is still, from purely earthly necessities, obliged to eat and drink and, in fact, submit to human requirements. Learn, my charming child, blessed as you are with absence of knowledge, that the depths of the earth, and the air, water, and fire, are filled with spiritual beings of higher and yet of more restricted nature than mankind. It seems unnecessary, my little unwise one, to explain to you the peculiar nature and characteristics of the gnomes, the salamanders, sylphides, and undines; you would not be able to understand them. To give you some slight idea of the danger which you may be undergoing, it is sufficient that I should tell you that these spirits are always striving eagerly to enter into unions with human beings; and as they are well aware that human beings are strongly adverse to those unions, they employ all manner of subtle and crafty artifices to delude such of the latter as they have fixed their affections upon. Often it is a twig, a flower, a glass of water, a fire-steel, or something else, in appearance of no importance, which they employ as a means of compassing their intent. It is true that unions of this sort often turn out exceedingly happily, as in the case of two priests, mentioned by Prince della Mirandola, who spent forty years of the happiest possible wedlock with a spirit of this description. It is true, moreover, that the most renowned sages have been the offspring of such unions between human beings and elementary spirits. Thus, the great Zoroaster was a son of the salamander Oromasis; the great Apollonius, the sage Merlin, the valiant Count of Cleve, and the great cabbalist, Ben-Syra, were the glorious fruits of marriages of this description, and according to Paracelsus the beautiful Melusina was no other than a sylphide. But yet, notwithstanding, the peril of such a union is much too great, for not only do the elementary spirits require of those on whom they confer their favours that the clearest light of the profoundest wisdom shall have arisen and shall shine upon them, but besides this they are extraordinarily touchy and sensitive, and revenge offences with extreme severity. Thus, it once happened that a sylphide, who was in union with a philosopher, on an occasion when he was talking with friends about a pretty woman--and perhaps rather too warmly--suddenly allowed her white beautifully-formed limb to become visible in the air, as if to convince the friends of her beauty, and then killed the poor philosopher on the spot. But ah! why should I refer to others? Why don't

I speak of myself? I am aware that for the last twelve years I have been beloved by a sylphide, but she is timorous and coy, and I am tortured by the thought of the danger of fettering her to me more closely by cabbalistic processes, inasmuch as I am still much too dependent on earthly necessities, and consequently lack the necessary degree of wisdom. Every morning I make up my mind to fast, and I succeed in letting breakfast pass without touching any; but when mid-day comes, oh! Anna, my daughter Anna, you know well that I eat tremendously."

These latter words Herr Dapsul uttered almost in a howl, while bitter tears rolled down his lean chop-fallen cheeks. He then went on more calmly--

"But I take the greatest of pains to behave towards the elementary spirit who is thus favourably disposed towards me with the utmost refinement of manners, the most exquisite galanterie. I never venture to smoke a pipe of tobacco without employing the proper preliminary cabbalistic precautions, for I cannot tell whether or not my tender air-spirit may like the brand of the tobacco, and so be annoyed at the defilement of her element. And I take the same precautions when I cut a hazel twig, pluck a flower, eat a fruit, or strike fire, all my efforts being directed to avoid giving offence to any elementary spirit. And yet--there, you see that nutshell, which I slid upon, and, falling over backwards, completely nullified the whole important experiment, which would have revealed to me the whole mystery of the ring? I do not remember that I have ever eaten a nut in this chamber, completely devoted as it is to science (you know now why I have my breakfast on the stairs), and it is all the clearer that some little gnome must have been hidden away in that shell, very likely having come here to prosecute his studies, and watch some of my experiments. For the elementary spirits are fond of human science, particularly such kinds of it as the uninitiated vulgar consider to be, if not foolish and superstitious, at all events beyond the powers of the human mind to comprehend, and for that reason style 'dangerous.' Thus, when I accidentally trod upon this little student's head, I suppose he got in a rage, and threw me down. But it is probable that he had a deeper reason for preventing me from finding out the secret of the ring. Anna, my dear Anna, listen to this. I had ascertained that there is a gnome bestowing his favour upon you, and to judge by the ring he must be a gnome of rank and distinction, as well as of superior cultivation. But, my dear Anna, my most beloved little stupid girl, how do you suppose you are going to enter into any kind of union with an elementary spirit without running the most terrible risk? If you had read Cassiodorus Remus you might, of course, reply that, according to his veracious chronicle, the celebrated Magdalena de la Croix, abbess of a convent at Cordova, in Spain, lived for thirty years in the happiest wedlock imaginable with a little gnome, whilst a similar result followed in the case of a sylph and the young Gertrude, a nun in Kloster Nazareth, near Cologne. But, then, think of the learned pursuits of those ecclesiastical ladies and of your own; what a mighty difference. Instead of reading in learned books you are often employing your time in feeding hens, geese, ducks, and other creatures, which simply molest and annoy all cabbalists; instead of watching the course of the stars, the heavens, you dig in the earth; instead of deciphering the traces of the future in skilfully-constructed horoscopes you are churning milk into butter, and putting sauerkraut up to pickle for mean everyday winter use; although, really, I must say that for my own part I should be very sorry to be without such articles of food. Say, is all this likely, in the long run, to content a refined philosophic elementary spirit? And then, oh Anna! it must be through you that the Dapsulheim line must continue, which earthly demand upon your being you cannot refuse to obey in any possible case. Yet, in connection with this ring, you in your instinctive way felt a strange irreflective sense of physical enjoyment. By means of the operation in which I was engaged, I desired and intended to break the power of the ring, and free you entirely from the gnome which is pursuing you. That operation failed, in consequence of the trick played me by the little student in the nut-shell. And yet, notwithstanding, I feel inspired by a courage such as I never felt before to do battle with this elementary spirit. You are my child, whom I begot, not indeed with a sylphide, salamandress, or other elementary spirit, but of that poor country lady of a fine old family, to whom the God-forgotten neighbours gave the nickname of the 'goat-girl' on account of her idyllic nature. For she used to go out with a flock of pretty little white goats, and pasture them on the green hillocks, I meanwhile blowing a reed-pipe on my tower, a love-stricken young fool, by way of accompaniment. Yes, you are my own child, my flesh and blood, and I mean to rescue you. Here, this mystic file shall befree you from the pernicious ring."

With this, Herr Dapsul von Zabelthau took up a small file and began filing away with it at the ring. But scarcely had he passed it once or twice backwards and forwards when Fräulein Aennchen cried aloud in pain, "Papa, papa, you're filing my finger off!" And actually there was dark thick blood coming oozing from under the ring. Seeing this, Herr Dapsul let the file fall upon the floor, sank half fainting into the armchair, and cried, in utter despair, "Oh--oh--oh--oh! It is all over with me! Perhaps the infuriated gnome may come this very hour and bite my head off unless the sylphide saves me. Oh, Anna, Anna, go--fly!"

As her father's extraordinary talk had long made her wish herself far enough away, she ran downstairs like the wind.

CHAPTER III.

SOME ACCOUNT IS GIVEN OF THE ARRIVAL OF A REMARKABLE PERSONAGE IN DAPSULHEIM, AND OF WHAT FOLLOWED FURTHER.

Herr Dapsul Von Zabelthau had just embraced his daughter with many tears, and was moving off to ascend his tower, where he dreaded every moment the alarming visit of the incensed gnome, when the sound of a horn, loud and clear, made itself heard, and into the courtyard came bounding and curvetting a little cavalier of sufficiently strange and amusing appearance. His yellow horse was not at all large, and was of delicate build, so that the little rider, in spite of his large shapeless head, did not look so dwarfish as might otherwise have been the case, as he sate a considerable height above the horse's head. But this was attributable to the length of his body, for what of him hung over the saddle in the nature of legs and feet was hardly worth mentioning. For the rest, the little fellow had on a very rich habit of gold-yellow atlas, a fine high cap with a splendid grass-green plume, and riding-boots of beautifully polished mahogany. With a resounding "P-r-r-r-r-r!" he reined up before Herr von Zabelthau, and seemed to be going to dismount. But he suddenly slipped under the horse's belly as quick as lightning, and having got to the other side of him, threw himself three times in succession some twelve ells up in the air, turning six somersaults in every ell, and then alighted on his head in the saddle. Standing on his head there, he galloped backwards, forwards, and sideways in all sorts of extraordinary curves and ups and downs, his feet meanwhile playing trochees, dactyls, pyrrhics, &c., in the air. When this accomplished gymnast and trick-act rider at length stood still, and politely saluted, there were to be seen on the ground of the courtyard the words, "My most courteous greeting to you and your lady daughter, most highly respected Herr Dapsul von Zabelthau." These words he had ridden into the ground in handsome Roman uncial letters. Thereupon, he sprang from his horse, turned three Catherine wheels, and said that he was charged by his gracious master, the Herr Baron Porphyrio von Ockerodastes, called "Cordovanspitz," to present his compliments to Herr Dapsul von Zabelthau, and to say, that if the latter had no objection, the Herr Baron proposed to pay him a friendly visit of a day or two, as he was expecting presently to be his nearest neighbour.

Herr Dapsul looked more dead than alive, so pale and motionless did he stand, leaning un his daughter. Scarcely had a half involuntary, "It--will--give--me--much--pleasure," escaped his trembling lips, when the little horseman departed with lightning speed, and similar ceremonies to those with which he had arrived.

"Ah, my daughter!" cried Herr Dapsul, weeping and lamenting, "alas! it is but too certain that this is the gnome come to carry you off, and twist my unfortunate neck. But we will pluck up the very last scrap of courage which we can scrape together. Perhaps it may be still possible to pacify this irritated elementary spirit. We must be as careful in our conduct towards him as ever we can. I will at once read to you, my dear child, a chapter or two of Lactantius or Thomas Aquinas concerning the mode of dealing with elementary spirits, so that you mayn't make some tremendous mistake or other."

But before he could go and get hold of Lactantius or Thomas Aquinas, a band was heard in the immediate proximity, sounding very much like the kind of performance which children who are musical enough get up about Christmas-time. And a fine long procession was coming up the street. At the head of it rode some sixty or seventy little cavaliers on little yellow horses, all dressed like the one who had arrived as avant-courier at first, in yellow habits, pointed caps, and boots of polished mahogany. They were followed by a couch of purest crystal, drawn by eight yellow horses, and behind this came well on to forty other less magnificent coaches, some with six horses, some with only four. And there were swarms of pages, running footmen, and other attendants, moving up and down amongst and around those coaches in brilliant costumes, so that the whole thing formed a sight as charming as uncommon. Herr Dapsul stood sunk in gloomy amazement. Aennchen, who had never dreamt that the world could contain such lovely delightful creatures as these little horses and people, was quite out of her senses with delight, and forgot everything, even to shut her mouth, which she had opened to emit a cry of joy.

The coach and eight drew up before Herr Dapsul. Riders jumped from their horses, pages and attendants came hurrying forward, and the personage who was now lifted down the steps of the coach on their arms was none other than the Herr Baron Porphyrio von Ockerodastes, otherwise known as Cordovanspitz. Inasmuch as regarded his figure, the Herr Baron was far from comparable to the Apollo of Belvedere, or even the Dying Gladiator. For, besides the circumstances that he was scarcely three feet high, one-third of his small body consisted of his evidently too large and broad head, which was, moreover, adorned by a tremendously long Roman nose and a pair of great round projecting eyes. And as his body was disproportionately long for his height, there was nothing left for his legs and feet to occupy but some four inches or so. This small space was made the most of, however, for the little Baron's feet were the neatest and prettiest little things ever beheld. No doubt they seemed to be scarcely strong enough to support the large, important head. For the Baron's gait was somewhat tottery and uncertain, and he even toppled over altogether pretty frequently, but got up upon his feet immediately, after the manner of a jack-in-the-box. So that this toppling over had a considerable resemblance to some rather eccentric dancing step more than to anything else one could compare it to. He had on a close-fitting suit of some shining gold fabric, and a headdress, which was almost like a crown, with an enormous plume of green feathers in it.

As soon as the Baron had alighted on the ground, he hastened up to Herr Dapsul von Zabelthau, took hold of both his hands, swung himself up to his neck, and cried out, in a voice wonderfully more powerful than his shortness of stature would have led one to expect, "Oh, my Dapsul von Zabelthau, my most beloved father!" He then lowered himself down from Herr Dapsul's neck with the same deftness of skill with which he had climbed up to it, sprang, or rather slung himself, to Fräulein Aennchen, took that hand of hers which had the ring on it, covered it with loud resounding kisses, and cried out in the same almost thundering voice as before, "Oh, my loveliest Fräulein Anna von Zabelthau, my most beloved bride-elect!"

He then clapped his hands, and immediately that noisy clattering child-like band struck up, and over a hundred little fellows, who had got off their horses and out of the carriages, danced as the avant-courier had done, sometimes on their heads, sometimes on their feet, in the prettiest possible trochees, spondees, iambics, pyrrhics, anapaests, tribrachs, bacchi, antibacchi, choriambs, and dactyls, so that it was a joy to behold them. But as this was going on, Fräulein Aennchen recovered from the terrible fright which the little Baron's speech to her had put her in, and entered into several important and necessary economic questions and considerations. "How is it possible," she asked herself, "that these little beings can find room in this place of ours? Would it hold even their servants if they were to be put to sleep in the big barn? Then what could I do with the swell folk who came in the coaches, and of course expect to be put into fine bedrooms, with soft beds, as they're accustomed to be? And even if the two plough horses were to go out of the stable, and I were to be so hard hearted as to turn the old lame chestnut out into the grass field, would there be anything like room enough for all those little beasts of horses that this nasty ugly Baron has brought? And just the same with the one and forty coaches. But the worst of all comes after that. Oh, my gracious! is the whole year's provender anything like enough to keep all these little creatures going for even so much as a couple of days?" This last was the climax of all. She saw in her mind's eye everything eaten up--all the new vegetables, the sheep, the poultry, the salt meat--nay, the very beetroot brandy gone. And this brought the salt tears to her eyes. She thought she caught the Baron making a sort of wicked impudent face at her, and that gave her courage to say to him (while his people were keeping up their dancing with might and main), in the plainest language possible, that however flattering his visit might be to her father, it was impossible to think of such a thing as its lasting more than a couple of hours or so, as there was neither room nor anything else for the proper reception and entertainment of such a grand gentleman and such a numerous retinue. But little Cordovanspitz immediately looked as marvellously sweet and tender as any marsipan tart, pressing with closed eyes Fräulein Aennchen's hand (which was rather rough, and not particularly white) to his lips, as he assured her that the last thing he should think of was causing the dear papa and his lovely daughter the slightest inconvenience. He said he had brought everything in the kitchen and cellar department with him, and as for the lodging, he needed nothing but a little bit of ground with the open air above it, where his people could put up his ordinary travelling palace, which would accommodate him, his whole retinue, and the animals pertaining to them.

Fräulein Aennchen was so delighted with these words of the Baron Porphyrio von Ockerodastes that, to show that she wasn't grudging a little bit of hospitality, she was going to offer him the little fritter cakes she had made for the last consecration day, and a small glass of the beetroot brandy, unless he would have preferred double bitters, which the maid had brought from the town and recommended as strengthening to the stomach. But at this moment Cordovanspitz announced that he had chosen the kitchen garden as the site of his palace, and Aennchen's happiness was gone. But whilst the Baron's retainers, in celebration of their lord's arrival at Dapsulheim, continued their Olympian games, sometimes butting with their big heads at each other's stomachs, knocking each other over backwards, sometimes springing up in the air again, playing at skittles, being themselves in turn skittles, balls, and players, and so forth, Baron Porphyrio von Ockerodastes got into a very deep and interesting conversation with Herr Dapsul von Zabelthau, which seemed to go on increasing in importance till they went away together hand in hand, and up into the astronomical tower.

Full of alarm and anxiety, Fräulein Aennchen now made haste to her kitchen garden, with the view of trying to save whatever it might still be possible to save. The maid-servant was there already, standing staring before her with open mouth, motionless as a person turned like Lot's wife into a pillar of salt. Aennchen at once fell into the same condition beside her. At last they both cried out, making the welkin ring, "Oh, Herr Gemini! What a terrible sort of thing!" For the whole beautiful vegetable garden was turned into a wilderness. Not the trace of a plant in it, it looked like a devastated country.

"No," cried the maid, "there's no other way of accounting for it, these cursed little creatures have done it. Coming here in their coaches, forsooth! coaches, quotha! as if they were people of quality! Ha! ha! A lot of kobolds, that's what they are, trust me for that, Miss. And if I had a drop of holy water here I'd soon show you what all those fine things of theirs would turn to. But if they come here, the little brutes, I'll bash the heads of them with this spade here." And she flourished this threatening spade over her head, whilst Anna wept aloud.

But at this point, four members of Cordovanspitz's suite came up with such very pleasant ingratiating speeches and such courteous reverences, being such wonderful creatures to behold, at the same time that the maid, instead of attacking them with the spade, let it slowly sink, and Fräulein Aennchen ceased weeping.

They announced themselves as being the four friends who were the most immediately attached to their lord's person, saying that they belonged to four different nationalities (as their dress indicated, symbolically, at all events), and that their names were, respectively, Pan Kapustowicz, from Poland; Herr von Schwartzrettig, from Pomerania; Signor di Broccoli, from Italy; and Monsieur de Rocambolle, from France. They said, moreover, that the builders would come directly, and afford the beautiful lady the gratification of seeing them erect a lovely palace, all of silk, in the shortest possible space of time.

"What good will the silken palace be to me?" cried Fräulein Aennchen, weeping aloud in her bitter sorrow. "And what do I care about your Baron Cordovanspitz, now that you have gone and destroyed my beautiful vegetables, wretched creatures that you are. All my happy days are over."

But the polite interlocutors comforted her, and assured her that they had not by any means had the blame of desolating the kitchen-garden, and that, moreover, it would very soon be growing green and flourishing in such luxuriance as she had never seen, or anybody else in the world for that matter.

The little building-people arrived, and then there began such a confused-looking, higgledy-piggledy, and helter-skeltering on the plot of ground that Fräulein Anna and the maid ran away quite frightened, and took shelter behind some thickets, whence they could see what would be the end of it all.

But though they couldn't explain to themselves how things perfectly canny could come about as they did, there certainly arose and formed itself before their eyes, and in a few minutes' time, a lofty and magnificent marquee, made of a golden-yellow material and ornamented with many-coloured garlands and plumes, occupying the whole extent of the vegetable garden, so that the cords of it went right away over the village and into the wood beyond, where they were made fast to sturdy trees.

As soon as this marquee was ready, Baron Porphyrio came down with Herr Dapsul from the astronomical tower, after profuse embraces resumed his seat in the coach and eight, and in the same order in which they had made their entry into Dapsulheim, he and his following went into the silken palace, which, when the last of the procession was within it, instantly closed itself up.

Fräulein Aennchen had never seen her papa as he was then. The very faintest trace of the melancholy which had hitherto always so distressed him had completely disappeared from his countenance. One would really almost have said he smiled. There was a sublimity about his facial expression such as sometimes indicates that some great and unexpected happiness has come upon a person. He led his daughter by the hand in silence into the house, embraced her three times consecutively, and then broke out--

"Fortunate Anna! Thrice happy girl! Fortunate father! Oh, daughter, all sorrow and melancholy, all solicitude and misgiving are over for ever! Yours is a fate such as falls to the lot of few mortals. This Baron Porphyrio von Ockerodastes, otherwise known as Cordovanspitz, is by no means a hostile gnome, although he is descended from one of those elementary spirits who, however, was so fortunate as to purify his nature by the teaching of Oromasis the Salamander. The love of this being was bestowed upon a daughter of the human race, with whom he formed a union, and became founder of the most illustrious family whose name ever adorned a parchment. I have an impression that I told you before, beloved daughter Anna, that the pupil of the great Salamander Oromasis, the noble gnome Tsilmenech (a Chaldean name, which interpreted into our language has a somewhat similar significance to our word 'Thickhead'), bestowed his affection on the celebrated Magdalena de la Croix, abbess of a convent at Cordova in Spain, and lived in happy wedlock with her for nearly thirty years. And a descendant of the sublime family of higher intelligences which sprung from this union is our dear Baron Porphyrio von Ockerodastes, who has adopted the sobriquet of Cordovanspitz to indicate his ancestral connection with Cordova in Spain, and to distinguish himself by it from a more haughty but less worthy collateral line of the family, which bears the title of 'Saffian.' That a 'spitz' has been added to the 'Cordovan' doubtless possesses its own elementary astrological causes; I have not as yet gone into that subject. Following the example of his illustrious ancestor the gnome Tsilmenech, this splendid Ockerodastes of ours fell in love with you when you were only twelve years of age (Tsilmenech had done precisely the same thing in the case of Magdalena de la Croix). He was fortunate enough at that time to get a small gold ring from you, and now you wear his, so that your betrothal is indissoluble."

"What?" cried Fräulein Aennchen, in fear and amazement.

"What? I betrothed to him--I to marry that horrible little kobold? Haven't I been engaged for ever so long to Herr Amandus von Nebelstern? No, never will I have that hideous monster of a wizard for a husband. I don't care whether he comes from Cordova or from Saffian."

"There," said Herr Dapsul von Zabelthau more gravely, "there I perceive, to my sorrow and distress, how impossible it is for celestial wisdom to penetrate into your hardened, obdurate, earthly sense. You stigmatize this noble, elementary, Porphyrio von Ockerodastes as 'horrible' and 'ugly,' probably, I presume, because he is only three feet high, and, with the exception of his head, has very little worth speaking of on his body in the shape of arms, legs, and other appurtenances; and a foolish, earthly goose, such as you probably think of as to be admired, can't have legs long enough, on account of coat tails. Oh, my daughter, in what a terrible misapprehension you are involved! All beauty lies in wisdom, in the thought; and the physical symbol of thought is the head. The more head, the more beauty and wisdom. And if mankind could but cast away all the other members of the body as pernicious articles of luxury tending to evil, they would reach the condition of a perfect ideal of the highest type. Whence come all trouble and difficulty, vexation and annoyance, strife and contention--in short, all the depravities and miseries of humanity, but from the accursed luxury and voluptuousness of the members? Oh, what joy, what peace, what blessedness there would be on earth if the human race could exist without arms or legs, or the nether parts of the body--in short, if we were nothing but busts! Therefore it is a happy idea of the sculptors when they represent great statesmen, or celebrated men of science and learning as busts, symbolically indicating the higher nature within them. Wherefore, my daughter Anna, no more of such words as 'ugly and abominable' applied to the noblest of spirits, the grand Porphyrio von Ockerodastes, whose bride elect you most indubitably are. I must just tell you, at the same time, that by his important aid your father will soon attain that highest step of bliss towards which he has so long been striving. Porphyrio von Ockerodastes is in possession of authentic information that I am beloved by the sylphide Nehabilah (which in Syriac has very much the signification of our expression 'Peaky nose'), and he has promised to assist me to the utmost of his power to render myself worthy of a union with this higher spiritual nature. I have no doubt whatever, my dear child, that you will be well satisfied with your future stepmother. All I hope is, that a favourable destiny may so order matters that our marriages may both take place at one and the same fortunate hour."

Having thus spoken, Herr Dapsul von Zabelthau, casting a significant glance at his daughter, very pathetically left the room.

It was a great weight on Aennchen's heart that she remembered having, a great while ago, really in some unaccountable way lost a little gold ring, such as a child might wear, from her finger. So that it really seemed too certain that this abominable little wizard of a creature had indeed got her immeshed in his net, so that she couldn't see how she was

45

ever to get out of it. And over this she fell into the utmost grief and bewilderment. She felt that her oppressed heart must obtain relief; and this took place through the medium of a goose-quill, which she seized, and at once wrote off to Herr Amandus von Nebelstern as follows:

"My dearest Amandus--

"All is over with me completely. I am the most unfortunate creature in the whole world, and I'm sobbing and crying for sheer misery so terribly that the dear dumb animals themselves are sorry for me. And you'll be still sorrier than they are, because it's just as great a misfortune for you as it is for me, and you can't help being quite as much distressed about it as I am myself. You know that we love one another as fondly as any two lovers possibly can, and that I am betrothed to you, and that papa was going with us to the church. Very well. All of a sudden a nasty little creature comes here in a coach and eight, with a lot of people and servants, and says I have changed rings with him, and that he and I are engaged. And--just fancy how awful! papa says as well, that I must marry this little wretch, because he belongs to a very grand family. I suppose be very likely does, judging by his following and the splendid dresses they have on. But the creature has such a horrible name that, for that alone if it were for nothing else, I never would marry him. I can't even pronounce the heathenish words of the name; but one of them is Cordovanspitz, and it seems that is the family name. Write and tell me if these Cordovanspitzes really are so very great and aristocratic a family--people in the town will be sure to know if they are. And the things papa takes in his head at his time of life I really can't understand; but he wants to marry again, and this nasty Cordovanspitz is going to get him a wife that flies in the air. God protect us! Our servant girl is looking over my shoulder, and says she hasn't much of an opinion of ladies who can fly in the air and swim in the water, and that she'll have to be looking out for another situation, and hopes, for my sake, that my stepmother may break her neck the first time she goes riding through the air to St. Walpurgis. Nice state of things, isn't it? But all my hope is in you. For I know you are the person who ought to be, and has got to be, just where and what you are, and has to deliver me from a great danger. The danger has come, so be quick, and rescue

"Your grieved to death, but most true and loving fiancée,

"Anna von Zabelthau.

"P.S.--Couldn't you call this yellow little Cordovanspitz out? I'm sure you could settle his hash. He's feeble on his legs.

"What I implore you to do is to put on your things as fast as you can and hasten to

"Your most unfortunate and miserable,

"But always most faithful fiancée.

"Anna von Zabelthau."

CHAPTER IV.

IN WHICH THE HOUSEHOLD STATE OF A GREAT KING IS DESCRIBED; AND AFTERWARDS A BLOODY DUEL AND OTHER REMARKABLE OCCURRENCES ARE TREATED OF.

Fräulein Aennchen was so miserable and distressed that she felt paralyzed in all her members. She was sitting at the window with folded arms gazing straight before her, heedless of the cackling, crowing, and queaking of the fowls, which couldn't understand why on earth she didn't come and drive them into their roosts as usual, seeing that the twilight was coming on fast. Nay, she sat there with perfect indifference and allowed the maid to carry out this duty, and to hit the big cock (who opposed himself to the state of things and evinced decided resistance to her authority) a good sharp whang with her whip. For the love-pain which was rending her own heart was making her indifferent to the troubles of the dear pupils of her happier hours--those which she devoted to their up-bringing, although she had never studied Chesterfield or Knigge, or consulted Madame de Genlis, or any of those other authorities on the mental culture of the young, who know to a hair's-breadth exactly how they ought to be moulded. In this respect she really had laid herself open to censure on the score of lack of due seriousness.

All that day Cordovanspitz had not shown himself, but had been shut up in the tower with Herr Dapsul, no doubt assisting in the carrying on of important operations. But now Fräulein Aennchen caught sight of the little creature coming tottering across the courtyard in the glowing light of the setting sun. And it struck her that he looked more hideous in that yellow habit of his than he had ever done before. The ridiculous manner in which he went wavering about, jumping here and there, seeming to topple over every minute and then pick himself up again (at which anybody else would have died of laughing), only caused her the bitterer distress. Indeed, she at last held her hands in front of her eyes, that she mightn't so much as see the little horrid creature at all. Suddenly she felt something tugging at her dress, and cried "Down, Feldmann!" thinking it was the Dachshund. But it was not the dog; and what Fräulein Aennchen saw when she took her hands from her eyes was the Herr Baron Porphyrio von Ockerodastes, who hoisted himself into her lap with extraordinary deftness, and clasped both his arms about her. She screamed aloud with fear and disgust, and started up from her chair. But Cordovanspitz kept clinging on to her neck, and instantly became so wonderfully heavy that he seemed to weigh a ton at least, and he dragged the unfortunate Aennchen back again into her chair. Having got her there, however, he slid down out of her lap, sank on one knee as gracefully as possible, and as prettily as his weakness in the direction of equilibrium permitted, and said, in a clear voice--rather peculiar, but by no means unpleasing: "Adored Anna von Zabelthau, most glorious of ladies, most choice of brides-elect; no anger, I implore, no anger, no anger. I know you think my people laid waste your beautiful vegetable garden to put up my palace. Oh, powers of the universe, if you could but look into this little body of mine which throbs with magnanimity and love; if you could but detect all the cardinal virtues which are collected in my breast, under this yellow Atlas habit. Oh, how guiltless am I of the shameful cruelty which you attribute to me! How could a beneficent prince treat in such a way his very own subjects. But hold-- hold! What are words, phrases? You must see with your own eyes, my betrothed, the splendours which attend you. You must come with me at once. I will lead you to my palace, where a joyful people await the arrival of her who is beloved by their lord."

It may be imagined how terrified Fräulein Aennchen was at this proposition of Cordovanspitz's, and how hard she tried to avoid going so much as a single step with the little monster. But he continued to describe the extraordinary beauty and the marvellous richness of the vegetable garden which was his palace, in such eloquent and persuasive language, that at last she thought she would just have a peep into the marquee, as that couldn't do her much harm. The little creature, in his joy and delight, turned at least twelve Catherine wheels in succession, and then took her hand with much courtesy, and led her through the garden to the silken palace.

With a loud "Ah!" Fräulein Aennchen stood riveted to the ground with delight when the curtains of the entrance drew apart, displaying a vegetable garden stretching away further than the eye could reach, of such marvellous beauty and luxuriance as was never seen in the loveliest dreams. Here there was growing and flourishing every thing in the nature of colewort, rape, lettuce, pease and beans, in such a shimmer of light, and in such luxuriance that it is impossible to describe it. A band of pipes, drums and cymbals sounded louder, and the four gentlemen whose acquaintance she had previously made, viz. Herr von Schwartzrettig, Monsieur de Rocambolle, Signor di Broccoli and Pan Kapustowicz, approached with many ceremonious reverences.

"My chamberlains," said Porphyrio von Ockerodastes, smiling; and, preceded by them, he conducted Fräulein Aennchen through between the double ranks of the bodyguard of Red English Carrots to the centre of the plain, where stood a splendid throne. And around this throne were assembled the grandees of the realm; the Lettuce Princes with the Bean Princesses, the Dukes of Cucumber with the Prince of Melon at their head, the Cabbage Minister, the General Officer of Onions and Carrots, the Colewort ladies, etc., etc., all in the gala dresses of their rank and station. And amidst them moved up and down well on to a hundred of the prettiest and most delightful Lavender and Fennel pages, diffusing sweet perfume. When Ockerodastes had ascended the throne with Fräulein Aennchen, Chief Court-Marshal Turnip waved his long wand of office, and immediately the band stopped playing, and the multitude listened in reverential silence as Ockerodastes raised his voice and said, in solemn accents, "My faithful and beloved subjects, you see by my side the noble Fräulein Anna von Zabelthau, whom I have chosen to be my consort. Rich in beauty and virtues, she has long watched over you with the eye of maternal affection, preparing soft and succulent beds for you, caring for you and tending you with ceaseless ardour. She will ever be a true and befitting mother of this realm. Wherefore I call upon you to evince and give expression to the dutiful approval, and the duly regulated rejoicing at the favour and benefit which I am about to graciously confer upon you."

At a signal given by Chief Court-Marshal Turnip there arose the shout of a thousand voices, the Bulb Artillery fired their pieces, and the band of the Carrot Guard played the celebrated National Anthem--

"Salad and lettuce, and parsley so green."

It was a grand, a sublime moment, which drew tears from the eyes of the grandees, particularly from those of the Colewort ladies. Fräulein Aennchen, too, nearly lost all her self-control when she noticed that little Ockerodastes had a crown on his head all sparkling with diamonds, and a golden sceptre in his hand.

"Ah!" she cried clapping her hands. "Oh, Gemini! You seem to be something much grander than we thought, my dear Herr von Cordovanspitz."

"My adored Anna," he replied, "the stars compelled me to appear before your father under an assumed name. You must be told, dearest girl, that I am one of the mightiest of kings, and rule over a realm whose boundaries are not discoverable, as it has been omitted to lay them down in the maps. Oh, sweetest Anna, he who offers you his hand and crown is Daucus Carota the First, King of the Vegetables. All the vegetable princes are my vassals, save that the King of the Beans reigns for one single day in every year, in conformity to an ancient usage."

"Then I am to be a queen, am I?" cried Fräulein Aennchen, overjoyed. "And all this great splendid vegetable garden is to be mine?"

King Daucus assured her that of course it was to be so, and added that he and she would jointly rule over all the vegetables in the world. She had never dreamt of anything of the kind, and thought little Cordovanspitz wasn't anything like so nasty-looking as he used to be now that he was transformed into King Daucus Carota the First, and that the crown and sceptre were very becoming to him, and the kingly mantle as well. When she reckoned into the bargain his delightful manners, and the property this marriage would bring her, she felt certain that there wasn't a country lady in all the world who could have made a better match than she, who found herself betrothed to a king before she knew where she was. So she was delighted beyond measure, and asked her royal fiancé whether she could not take up her abode in the palace then and there, and be married next day. But King Daucus answered that eagerly as he longed for the time when he might call her his own, certain constellations compelled him to postpone that happiness a little longer. And that Herr Dapsul von Zabelthau, moreover, must be kept in ignorance of his son-in-law's royal station, because otherwise the operations necessary for bringing about the desired union with the sylphide Nehabilah might be unsuccessful. Besides, he said, he had promised that both the weddings should take place on the same day. So Fräulein Aennchen had to take a solemn vow not to mention one syllable to Herr Dapsul of what had been happening to her. She therefore left the silken palace amid long and loud rejoicings of the people, who were in raptures with her beauty as well as with her affability and gracious condescension of manners and behaviour.

In her dreams she once more beheld the realms of the charming King Daucus, and was lapped in Elysium.

The letter which she had sent to Herr Amandus von Nebelstern made a frightful impression on him. Ere long, Fräulein Aennchen received the following answer--

'Idol of my Heart, Heavenly Anna,--

"Daggers--sharp, glowing, poisoned, death-dealing daggers were to me the words of your letter, which pierced my breast through and through. Oh, Anna! you to be torn from me. What a thought! I cannot, even now, understand how it was that I did not go mad on the spot and commit some terrible deed. But I fled the face of man, overpowered with rage at my deadly destiny, after dinner--without the game of billiards which I generally play--out into the woods, where I wrung my hands, and called on your name a thousand times. It came on a tremendously heavy rain, and I had on a new cap, red velvet, with a splendid gold tassel (everybody says I never had anything so becoming). The rain was spoiling it, and it was brand-new. But what are caps, what are velvet and gold, to a despairing lover? I strode up and down till I was wet to the skin and chilled to the bone, and had a terrible pain in my stomach. This drove me into a restaurant near, where I got them to make me some excellent mulled wine, and had a pipe of your heavenly Virginia tobacco. I soon felt myself elevated on the wings of a celestial inspiration, took out my pocket-book, and, oh!--wondrous gift of poetry--the love-despair and the stomach-ache both disappeared at once. I shall content myself with writing out for you only the last of these poems; it will inspire you with heavenly hope, as it did myself.

"Wrapped in darkest sorrow--
In my heart, extinguished,
No love-tapers burning--
Joy hath no to-morrow.
"Ha! the Muse approaches,
Words and rhymes inspiring,
Little verse inscribing,
Joy returns apace.
"New love-tapers blazing,
All the heart inspiring,
Fare thee well, my sorrow,
Joy thy place doth borrow.

"Ay, my sweet Anna, soon shall I, thy champion, hasten to rescue you from the miscreant who would carry you off from me. So, once more take comfort, sweetest maid. Bear me ever in thy heart. He comes; he rescues you; he clasps you to his bosom, which heaves in tumultuous emotion.

"Your ever faithful

"Amandus von Nebelstern.

"P.S.--It would be quite impossible for me to call Herr von Cordovanspitz out. For, oh Anna! every drop of blood drawn from your Amandus by the weapon of a presumptuous adversary were glorious poet's blood--ichor of the gods-- which never ought to be shed. The world very properly claims that such a spirit as mine has it imposed upon it as public duty to take care of itself for the world's benefit, and preserve itself by every possible means. The sword of the poet is the word--the song. I will attack my rival with Tyrtæan battle- songs; strike him to earth with sharp-pointed epigrams; hew him down with dithyrambics full of lover's fury. Such are the weapons of a true, genuine poet, powerful to shield him from every danger. And it is so accoutred that I shall appear, and do battle--victorious battle--for your hand, oh, Anna!

"Farewell. I press you once more to my heart. Hope all things from my love, and, especially, from my heroic courage, which will shun no danger to set you free from the shameful nets of captivity in which, to all appearance, you are entangled by a demoniacal monster."

Fräulein Aennchen received this letter at a time when she was playing a game at "Catch-me-if-you-can" with her royal bridegroom elect, King Daucus Carota the First, in the meadow at the back of the garden, and immensely enjoying it when, as was often the case, she suddenly ducked down in full career, and the little king would go shooting right away over her head. Instead of reading the letter immediately (which she had always done before), she put it in her pocket unopened, and we shall presently see that it came too late.

Herr Dapsul could not make out at all how Fräulein Aennchen had changed her mind so suddenly, and grown quite fond of Herr Porphyrio von Ockerodastes, whom she had so cordially detested before. He consulted the stars on the subject, but as they gave him no satisfactory information, he was obliged to come to the conclusion that human hearts are more mysterious and inscrutable than all the secrets of the universe, and not to be thrown light upon by any constellation. He could not think that what had produced love for the little creature in Anna's heart was merely the highness of his nature; and personal beauty he had none. If (as the reader knows) the canon of beauty, as laid down by Herr Dapsul, is very unlike the ideas which young ladies form upon that subject, he did, after all, possess sufficient knowledge of the world to know that, although the said young women hold that good sense, wit, cleverness and pleasant manners are very agreeable fellow-lodgers in a comfortable house, still, a man who can't call himself the possessor of a properly-made, fashionable coat--were he a Shakespeare, a Goethe, a Tieck, or a Jean Paul Richter--would run a decided risk of being beaten out of the field by any sufficiently well put-together lieutenant of hussars in uniform, if he took it in his head to pay his addresses to one of them. Now in Fräulein Aennchen's case it was a different matter altogether. It was neither good looks nor cleverness that were in question; but it is not exactly every day that a poor country lady becomes a queen all in a moment, and accordingly it was not very likely that Herr Dapsul should hit upon the cause which had been operating, particularly as the very stars had left him in the lurch.

As may be supposed, those three, Herr Porphyrio, Herr Dapsul and Fräulein Aennchen, were one heart and one soul. This went so far that Herr Dapsul left his tower oftener than he had ever been known to do before, to chat with his much-prized son-in-law on all sorts of agreeable subjects; and not only this, but he now regularly took his breakfast in the house. About this hour, too, Herr Porphyrio was wont to come forth from his silken palace, and eat a good share of Fräulein Aennchen's bread and butter.

"Ah, ah!" she would often whisper softly in his ear, "if papa only knew that you are a real king, dearest Cordovanspitz!"

"Be still, oh heart! Melt not away in rapture," Daucus Carota the First would say. "Near, near is the joyful day!"

It chanced that the schoolmaster had sent Fräulein Aennchen a present of some of the finest radishes from his garden. She was particularly pleased at this, as Herr Dapsul was very fond of radishes, and she could not get anything from the vegetable garden because it was covered by the silk marquee. Besides this, it now occurred to her for the first time that, among all the roots and vegetables she had seen in the palace, radishes were conspicuous by their absence.

So she speedily cleaned them and served them up for her father's breakfast. He had ruthlessly shorn several of them of their leafy crowns, dipped them in salt, and eaten them with much relish, when Cordovanspitz came in.

"Oh, my Ockerodastes," Herr Dapsul called to him, "are you fond of radishes?"

There was still a particularly fine and beautiful radish on the dish. But the moment Cordovanspitz saw it his eves gleamed with fury, and he cried in a resonant voice--

"What, unworthy duke, do you dare to appear in my presence again, and to force your way, with the coolest of audacity, into a house which is under my protection? Have I not pronounced sentence of perpetual banishment upon you as a pretender to the imperial throne? Away, treasonous vassal; begone from my sight for ever!"

Two little legs had suddenly shot out beneath the radish's large head, and with them he made a spring out of the plate, placed himself close in front of Cordovanspitz, and addressed him as follows--

"Fierce and tyrannical Daucus Carota the First, you have striven in vain to exterminate my race. Had ever any of your family a head as large as mine, or that of my king? We are all gifted with talent, common-sense, wisdom, sharpness, cultivated manners: and whilst you loaf about in kitchens and stables, and are of no use as soon as your early youth is gone (so that in very truth it is nothing but the diable de la jeunesse that bestows upon you your brief, transitory, little bit of good fortune), we enjoy the friendship of, and the intercourse with, people of position, and are greeted with acclamation as soon as ever we lift up our green heads.

59

But I despise you, Daucus Carota. You're nothing but a low, uncultivated, ignorant Boor, like all the lot of you. Let's see which of us two is the better man."

With this the Duke of Radish, flourishing a long whip about his head, proceeded, without more ado, to attack the person of King Daucus Carota the First. The latter quickly drew his little sword, and defended himself in the bravest manner. The two little creatures darted about in the room, fighting fiercely, and executing the most wonderful leaps and bounds, till Daucus Carota pressed the Duke of Radish so hard that the latter found himself obliged to make a tremendous jump out of the window and take to the open. But Daucus Carota--with whose remarkable agility and dexterity the reader is already acquainted--bounded out after him, and followed the Duke of Radish across country.

Herr Dapsul von Zabelthau had looked on at this terrible encounter rigid and speechless, but he now broke forth into loud and bitter lamentation, crying, "Oh, daughter Anna! oh, my poor unfortunate daughter Anna! Lost--I--you--both of us. All is over with us." With which he left the room, and ascended the astronomical tower as fast as his legs would carry him.

Fräulein Aennchen couldn't understand a bit, or form the very slightest idea what in all the world had set her father into all this boundless misery all of a sudden. The whole thing had caused her the greatest pleasure; moreover, her heart was rejoiced that she had had an opportunity of seeing that her future husband was brave, as well as rich and great;

for it would be difficult to find any woman in all the world capable of loving a poltroon. And now that she had proof of the bravery of King Daucus Carota the First, it struck her painfully, for the first time, that Herr Amandus von Nebelstern had cried off from fighting him. If she had for a moment hesitated about sacrificing Herr Amandus to King Daucus, she was quite decided on the point now that she had an opportunity of assuring herself of all the excellencies of her future lord. She sat down and wrote the following letter:--

"My dear Amandus,

"Everything in this world is liable to change. Everything passes away, as the schoolmaster says, and he's quite right. I'm sure you, my dear Amandus, are such a learned and wise student that you will agree with the schoolmaster, and not be in the very least surprised that my heart and mind have undergone the least little bit of a change. You may quite believe me when I say that I still like you very well, and I can quite imagine how nice you look in your red velvet cap with the gold tassel. But, with regard to marriage, you know very well, Amandus dear, that, clever as you are, and beautiful as are your verses, you will never, in all your days, be a king, and (don't be frightened, dear) little Herr von Cordovanspitz isn't Herr von Cordovanspitz at all, but a great king, Daucus Carota the First, who reigns over the great vegetable kingdom, and has chosen me to be his queen. Since my dear king has thrown aside his incognito he has grown much nicer-looking, and I see now that papa was quite right when he said that the head was the beauty of the man, and therefore couldn't possibly be big enough. And then, Daucus Carota the First (you see how well I remember the beautiful name and how nicely I write it now that has got so familiar to me), I was going to say that my little royal husband, that is to be, has such charming and delightful manners that there's no describing them. And what courage, what bravery there is in him! Before my eyes he put to flight the Duke of Radish, (and a very disagreeable, unfriendly creature he appears to be) and hey, how he did jump after him out of the window! You should just have seen him: I only wish you had! And I don't really think that my Daucus Carota would care about those weapons of yours that you speak about one bit. He seems pretty tough, and I don't believe verses would do him any harm at all, however fine and pointed they might be. So now, dear Amandus, you must just make up your mind to be contented with your lot, like a good fellow, and not be vexed with me that I am going to be a Queen instead of marrying you. Never mind, I shall always be your affectionate friend, and if ever you would like an appointment in the Carrot bodyguard, or (as you don't care so much about fighting as about learning) in the Parsley Academy or the Pumpkin Office, you have but to say the word and your fortune is made. Farewell, and don't be vexed with

"Your former fiancée, but now friend and well-wisher, as well as future Queen,

"Anna von Zabelthau.

"(but soon to be no more Von Zabelthau, but simply

ANNA.)

"P.S.--You shall always be kept well supplied with the very finest Virginia tobacco, of that you need have no fear. As far as I can see there won't be any smoking at my court, but I shall take care to have a bed or two of Virginia tobacco planted not far from the throne, under my own special care. This will further culture and morality, and my little Daucus will no doubt have a statute specially enacted on the subject."

CHAPTER V.

IN WHICH AN ACCOUNT IS GIVEN OF A FRIGHTFUL CATASTROPHE, AND WE PROCEED WITH THE FUTURE COURSE OF EVENTS.

Fräulein Aennchen had just finished her letter to Herr Amandus von Nebelstern, when in came Herr Dapsul von Zabelthau and began, in the bitterest grief and sorrow to say, "O, my daughter Anna, how shamefully we are both deceived and betrayed! This miscreant who made me believe he was Baron Porphyrio von Ockerodastes, known as Cordovanspitz, member of a most illustrious family descended from the mighty gnome Tsilmenech and the noble Abbess of Cordova--this miscreant, I say--learn it and fall down insensible--is indeed a gnome, but of that lowest of all gnomish castes which has charge of the vegetables. The gnome Tsilmenech was of the highest caste of all, that, namely, to which the care of the diamonds is committed. Next comes the caste which has care of the metals in the realms of the metal-king, and then follow the flower-gnomes, who are lower in position, as depending on the sylphs. But the lowest and most ignoble are the vegetable gnomes, and not only is this deceiver Cordovanspitz a gnome of this caste, but he is actual king of it, and his name is Daucus Carota."

Fräulein Aennchen was far from fainting away, neither was she in the smallest degree frightened, but she smiled in the kindliest way at her lamenting papa, and the Courteous

64

reader is aware of the reason. But as Herr Dapsul was very much surprised at this, and kept imploring her for Heaven's sake to realize the terrible position in which she was, and to feel the full horror of it, she thought herself at liberty to divulge the secret entrusted to her. She told Herr Dapsul how the so-called Baron von Cordovanspitz had told her his real position long ago, and that since then she had found him altogether so pleasant and delightful that she couldn't wish for a better husband. Moreover she described all the marvellous beauties of the vegetable kingdom into which King Daucus Carota the First had taken her, not forgetting to duly extol the remarkably delightful manners of the inhabitants of that realm.

Herr Dapsul struck his hands together several times, and wept bitterly over the deceiving wickedness of the Gnome-king, who had been, and still was, employing means the most artful--most dangerous for himself as well--to lure the unfortunate Anna down into his dark, demoniac kingdom. "Glorious," he explained, "glorious and advantageous as may be the union of an elementary spirit with a human being, grand as is the example of this given by the wedlock of the gnome Tsilmenech with Magdalena de la Croix (which is of course the reason why this deceiver Daucus Carota has given himself out as being a descendant of that union), yet the kings and princes of those races are very different. If the Salamander kings are only irascible, the sylph kings proud and haughty, the Undine queens affectionate and jealous, the gnome kings are fierce, cruel, and deceitful. Merely to revenge themselves on the children of earth, who deprive them of their vassals, they are constantly trying their utmost to lure one of them away, who then wholly lays aside her human nature, and, becoming as shapeless as the gnomes themselves, has to go down into the earth, and is never more seen."

Fräulein Aennchen didn't seem disposed to believe what her father was telling her to her dear Daucus's discredit, but began talking again about the marvels of the beautiful vegetable country over which she was expecting so soon to reign as queen.

"Foolish, blinded child," cried Herr Dapsul, "do you not give your father credit for possessing sufficient cabalistic science to be well aware that what the abominable Daucus Carota made you suppose you saw was all deception and falsehood? No, you don't believe me, and to save you, my only child, I must convince you, and this conviction must be arrived at by most desperate methods. Come with me."

For the second time she had to go up into the astronomical tower with her papa. From a big band-box Herr Dapsul took a quantity of yellow, red, white, and green ribbon, and, with strange ceremonies, he wrapped Fräulein Aennchen up in it from head to foot. He did the same to himself, and then they both went very carefully to the silken palace of Daucus Carota the First. It was close shut, and by her papa's directions, she had to rip a small opening in one of the seams of it with a large pair of scissors, and then peep in at the opening.

Heaven be about us! what did she see? Instead of the

beautiful vegetable garden, the carrot guards, the plumed ladies, lavender pages, lettuce princes, and so forth, she found herself looking down into a deep pool which seemed to be full of a colourless, disgusting-looking slime, in which all kinds of horrible creatures from the bowels of the earth were creeping and twining about. There were fat worms slowly writhing about amongst each other, and beetle-like creatures stretching out their short legs and creeping heavily out. On their backs they bore big onions; but these onions had ugly human faces, and kept fleering and leering at each other with bleared yellow eyes, and trying, with their little claws (which were close behind their ears), to catch hold of one another by their long roman noses, and drag each other down into the slime, while long, naked slugs were rolling about in crowds, with repulsive torpidity, stretching their long horns out of their depths. Fräulein Aennchen was nearly fainting away at this horrid sight. She held both hands to her face, and ran away as hard as she could.

"You see now, do you not," said Herr Dapsul, "how this atrocious Daucus Carota has been deceiving you in showing you splendours of brief duration? He dressed his vassals up in gala dresses to delude you with dazzling displays. But now you have seen the kingdom which you want to reign over in undress uniform; and when you become the consort of the frightful Daucus Carota you will have to live for ever in the subterranean realms, and never appear on the surface any more. And if--Oh, oh, what must I see, wretched, most miserable of fathers that I am?"

He got into such a state all in a moment that she felt certain some fresh misfortune had just come to light, and asked him anxiously what he was lamenting about now. However, he could do nothing for sheer sobbing, but stammer out, "Oh--oh--dau-gh-ter. Wha-t ar--e y-ou--l--l--like?" She ran to her room, looked into the looking-glass, and started back, terrified almost to death.

And she had reason; for the matter stood thus. As Herr Dapsul was trying to open the eyes of Daucus Carota's intended queen to the danger she was in of gradually losing her pretty figure and good looks, and growing more and more into the semblance of a gnome queen, he suddenly became aware of how far the process had proceeded already. Aennchen's head had got much broader and bigger, and her skin had turned yellow, so that she was quite ugly enough already. And though vanity was not one of her failings, she was woman enough to know that to grow ugly is the greatest and most frightful misfortune which can happen here below. How often had she thought how delightful it would be when she would drive, as queen, to church in the coach and eight, with the crown on her head, in satins and velvets, with diamonds, and gold chains, and rings, seated beside her royal husband, setting all the women, the schoolmaster's wife included, into amazement of admiration, and most likely, in fact, no doubt, instilling a proper sense of respect even into the minds of the pompous lord and lady of the manor themselves. Ay, indeed, how often had she been lapt in these and other such eccentric dreams, and visions of the future!--

Fräulein Aennchen burst into long and bitter weeping.

"Anna, my daughter Anna," cried Herr Dapsul down through the speaking trumpet; "come up here to me immediately!"

She found him dressed very much like a miner. He spoke in a tone of decision and resolution, saying, "When need is the sorest, help is often nearest. I have ascertained that Daucus Carota will not leave his palace to-day, and most probably not till noon of to-morrow. He has assembled the princes of his house, the ministers, and other people of consequence to hold a council on the subject of the next crop of winter cabbage. The sitting is important, and it may be prolonged so much that we may not have any cabbage at all next winter. I mean to take advantage of this opportunity, while he is so occupied with his official affairs that he won't be able to attend to my proceedings, to prepare a weapon with which I may perhaps attack this shameful gnome, and prevail over him, so that he will be compelled to withdraw, and set you at liberty. While I am at work, do you look uninterruptedly at the palace through this glass, and tell me instantly if anybody comes out, or even looks out of it." She did as she was directed, but the marquee remained closed, although she often heard (notwithstanding that Herr Dapsul was making a tremendous hammering on plates of metal a few paces behind her), a wild, confused crying and screaming, apparently coming from the marquee, and also distinct sounds of slapping, as if people's ears were being well boxed. She told Herr Dapsul this, and he was delighted, saying that the more they quarrelled in there the less they were likely to know what was being prepared for their destruction.

Fräulein Aennchen was much surprised when she found that Herr Dapsul had hammered out and made several most lovely kitchen-pots and stew-pans of copper. As an expert in such matters, she observed that the tinning of them was done in a most superior style, so that her papa must have paid careful heed to the duties legally enjoined on coppersmiths. She begged to be allowed to take these nice pots and pans down to the kitchen, and use them there. But Herr Dapsul smiled a mysterious smile, and merely said:

"All in good time, my daughter Anna. Just you go downstairs, my beloved child, and wait quietly till you see what happens to-morrow."

He gave a melancholy smile, and that infused a little hope and confidence into his luckless daughter.

Next day, as dinner-time came on, Herr Dapsul brought down his pots and pans, and betook himself to the kitchen, telling his daughter and the maid to go away and leave him by himself, as he was going to cook the dinner. He particularly enjoined Fräulein Aennchen to be as kind and pleasant with Cordovanspitz as ever she could, when he came in--as he was pretty sure to do.

Cordovanspitz--or rather, King Daucus Carota the First--did come in very soon, and if he had borne himself like an ardent lover on previous occasions, he far outdid himself on this. Aennchen noticed, to her terror, that she had grown so small by this time, that Daucus had no difficulty in getting

70

up into her lap to caress and kiss her; and the wretched girl had to submit to this, notwithstanding her disgust with the horrid little monster. Presently Herr Dapsul came in, and said--

"Oh, my most egregious Porphyrio von Ockerodastes, won't you come into the kitchen with my daughter and me, and see what beautiful order your future bride has got everything in there?"

Aennchen had never seen the wicked, malicious look upon her father's face before, which it wore when he took little Daucus by the arm, and almost forced him from the sitting-room to the kitchen. At a sign of her father's she went there after them.

Her heart swelled within her when she saw the fire burning so merrily, the glowing coals, the beautiful copper pots and pans. As Herr Dapsul drew Cordovanspitz closer to the fire-place, the hissing and bubbling in the pots grew louder and louder, and at last changed into whimpering and groaning. And out of one of the pots came voices, crying, "Oh Daucus Carota! Oh King, rescue your faithful vassals! Rescue us poor carrots! Cut up, thrown into despicable water; rubbed over with salt and butter to our torture, we suffer indescribable woe, whereof a number of noble young parsleys are partakers with us!"

And out of the pans came the plaint: "Oh Daucus Carota! Oh King! Rescue your faithful vassals--rescue us poor carrots. We are roasting in hell--and they put so little water with us, that our direful thirst forces us to drink our own heart's blood!"

And from another of the pots came: "Oh Daucus Carota! Oh King! Rescue your faithful vassals--rescue us poor carrots. A horrible cook eviscerated us, and stuffed our insides full of egg, cream, and butter, so that all our ideas and other mental qualities are in utter confusion, and we don't know ourselves what we are thinking about!"

And out of all the pots and pans came howling at once a general chorus of "Oh Daucus Carota! Mighty King! Rescue us, thy faithful vassals--rescue us poor carrots!"

On this, Cordovanspitz gave a loud, croaking cry of--"Cursed, infernal, stupid humbug and nonsense!" sprang with his usual agility on to the kitchen range, looked into one of the pots, and suddenly popped down into it bodily. Herr Dapsul sprang in the act of putting on the cover, with a triumphant cry of "a Prisoner!" But with the speed of a spiral spring Cordovanspitz came bounding up out of the pot, and gave Herr Dapsul two or three ringing slaps on the face, crying "Meddling goose of an old Cabalist, you shall pay for this! Come out, my lads, one and all!"

Then there came swarming out of all the pots and pans hundreds and hundreds of little creatures about the length of one's finger, and they attached themselves firmly all over Herr Dapsul's body, threw him down backwards into an enormous dish, and there dished him up, pouring the hot juice out of the pots and pans over him, and bestrewing him with chopped egg, mace, and grated breadcrumbs. Having done this, Daucus Carota darted out of the window, and his people after him.

Fräulein Aennchen sank down in terror beside the dish whereon her poor papa lay, served up in this manner as if for table. She supposed he was dead, as he gave not the faintest sign of life.

She began to lament: "Ah, poor papa--you're dead now, and there's nobody to save me from this diabolical Daucus!" But Herr Dapsul opened his eyes, sprang up from the dish with renewed energy, and cried in a terrible voice, such as she had never heard him make use of before, "Ah accursed Daucus Carota, I am not at the end of my resources yet. You shall soon see what the meddling old goose of a Cabalist can do."

Aennchen had to set to work and clean him with the kitchen besom from all the chopped egg, the mace, and the grated breadcrumbs; and then he seized a copper pot, crammed it on his head by way of a helmet, took a frying-pan in his left hand, and a long iron kitchen ladle in his right, and thus armed and accoutred, he darted out into the open. Fräulein Aennchen saw him running as hard as he could towards Cordovanspitz's marquee, and yet never moving from the same spot. At this her senses left her.

When she came to herself, Herr Dapsul had disappeared, and she got terribly anxious when evening came, and night, and even the next morning, without his making his appearance. She could not but dread the very worst.

CHAPTER VI.

WHICH IS THE LAST--AND, AT THE SAME TIME, THE MOST EDIFYING OF ALL.

Fräulein Aennchen was sitting in her room in the deepest sorrow, when the door opened, and who should come in but Herr Amandus von Nebelstern. All shame and contrition, she shed a flood of tears, and in the most weeping accents addressed him as follows: "Oh, my darling Amandus, pray forgive what I wrote to you in my blinded state! I was bewitched, and I am so still, no doubt. I am yellow, and I'm hideous, may God pity me! But my heart is true to you, and I am not going to marry any king at all."

"My dear girl," said Amandus, "I really don't see what you have to complain of. I consider you one of the luckiest women in the world."

"Oh, don't mock at me," she cried. "I am punished severely enough for my absurd vanity in wishing to be a Queen."

"Really and truly, my dear girl," said Amandus, "I can't make you out one bit. To tell you the real truth, your last letter drove me stark, staring mad. I first thrashed my servant-boy, then my poodle, smashed several glasses--and you know a student who's breathing out threatenings and slaughter in that sort of way isn't to be trifled with. But when I got a little calmer I made up my mind to come on here as quickly as I could, and see with my own eyes how, why, and to whom I had lost my intended bride. Love makes no distinction of class or station, and I made up my mind that I would make this King Daucus Carota give a proper account of himself, and ask him if this tale about his marrying you was mere brag, or if he really meant it--but everything here is different to what I expected. As I was passing near the grand marquee that is put up yonder, King Daucus Carota came out of it, and I soon found that I had before me the most charming prince I ever saw--at the same time he happens to be the first I ever did see; but that's nothing. For, just fancy, my dear girl, he immediately detected the sublime poet in me, praised my poems (which he has never read) above measure, and offered to appoint me Poet Laureate in his service. Now a position of that sort has long been the fairest goal of my warmest wishes, so that I accepted his offer with a thousandfold delight. Oh, my dear girl, with what an enthusiasm of inspiration will I chant your praises! A poet can love queens and princesses: or rather, it is really a part of his simple duty to choose a person of that exalted station to be the lady of his heart. And if he does get rather cracky in the head on the subject, that circumstance of itself gives rise to that celestial delirium without which no poetry is possible, and no one ought to feel any surprise at a poet's perhaps somewhat extravagant proceedings. Remember the great Tasso, who must have had a considerable bee in his bonnet when in love with the Princess Leonore d'Este. Yes, my dear girl, as you are going to be a queen so soon, you will always be the lady of my heart, and I will extol you to the stars in the sublimest and most celestial verses."

"What, you have seen him, the wicked Cobold?" Fräulein Aennchen broke out in the deepest amazement. "And he has----"

But at that moment in came the little gnomish King himself, and said, in the tenderest accents, "Oh, my sweet, darling fiancée! Idol of my heart! Do not suppose for a moment that I am in the least degree annoyed with the little piece of rather unseemly conduct which Herr Dapsul von Zabelthau was guilty of. Oh, no--and indeed it has led to the more rapid fulfilment of my hopes; so that the solemn ceremony of our marriage will actually be celebrated to-morrow. You will be pleased to find that I have appointed Herr Amandus von Nebelstern our Poet Laureate, and I should wish him at once to favour us with a specimen of his talents, and recite one of his poems. But let us go out under the trees, for I love the open air: and I will lie in your lap, while you, my most beloved bride elect, may scratch my head a little while he is singing--for I am fond of having my head scratched in such circumstances."

Fräulein Aennschen, turned to stone with horror and alarm, made no resistance to this proposal. Daucus Carota, out under the trees, laid himself in her lap, she scratched his head, and Herr Amandus, accompanying himself on the guitar, began the first of twelve dozen songs which he had composed and written out in a thick book.

It is matter of regret that in the Chronicle of Dapsulheim (from which all this history is taken), these songs have not been inserted, it being merely stated that the country folk who were passing, stopped on their way, and anxiously inquired who could be in such terrible pain in Herr Dapsul's wood, that he was crying and screaming out in such a style.

Daucus Carota, in Aennschen's lap, twisted and writhed, and groaned and whined more and more lamentably, as if he had a violent pain in his stomach. Moreover, Fräulein Aennchen fancied she observed, to her great amazement, that Cordovanspitz was growing smaller and smaller as the song went on. At last Herr Amandus sung the following sublime effusion (which is preserved in the Chronicle):--

"Gladly sings the Bard, enraptured,
Breath of blossoms, bright dream-visions,
Moving thro' roseate spaces in Heaven,
Blessed and beautiful, whither away?
'Whither away?' oh, question of questions--
Towards that 'Whither,' the Bard is borne onward,
Caring for nought but to love, to believe.
Moving through roseate heavenly spaces,
Towards this 'Whither,' where'er it may be,
Singeth the bard, in a tumult of rapture,
Ever becoming a radiant em----"

At this point, Daucus Carota uttered a loud croaking cry, and, now dwindled into a little, little carrot, slipped down from Aennchen's lap, and into the ground, leaving no trace behind. Upon which, the great grey fungus which had grown in the night time beside the grassy bank, shot up and up;

but this fungus was nothing less than Herr Dapsul von Zabelthau's grey felt hat, and he himself was under it, and fell stormily on Amandus's breast, crying out in the utmost ecstasy, "Oh, my dearest, best, most beloved Herr Amandus von Nebelstern, with that mighty song of conjuration you have beaten all my cabalistic science out of the field? What the profoundest magical art, the utmost daring of the philosopher fighting for his very existence, could not accomplish, your verses achieved, passing into the frame of the deceitful Daucus Carota like the deadliest poison, so that he must have perished of stomach-ache, in spite of his gnomish nature, if he had not made off into his kingdom. My daughter Anna is delivered--I am delivered from the horrible charm which held me spellbound here in the shape of a nasty fungus, at the risk of being hewn to pieces by my own daughter's hands; for the good soul hacks them all down with her spade, unless their edible character is unmistakable, as in the case of the mushrooms. Thanks, my most heartfelt thanks, and I have no doubt your intentions as regards my daughter have undergone no change. I am sorry to say she has lost her good looks, through the machinations of that inimical gnome; but you are too much of a philosopher to----"

"Oh, dearest papa," cried Aennchen, overjoyed; "just look there! The silken palace is gone! The abominable monster is off and away with all his tribe of salad-princes, cucumber-ministers, and Lord knows what all!" And she ran away to the vegetable garden, delighted, Herr Dapsul following as fast as he could. Herr Amandus went behind them, muttering to himself, "I'm sure I don't know quite what to make of all this. But this I maintain, that that ugly little carrot creature is a vile, prosaic lubber, and none of your poetical kings, or my sublime lay wouldn't have given him the stomach-ache, and sent him scuttling into the ground."

As Fräulein Aennchen was standing in the vegetable garden, where there wasn't the trace of a green blade to be seen, she suddenly felt a sharp pain in the finger which had on the fateful ring. At the same time a cry of piercing sorrow sounded from the ground, and the tip of a carrot peeped out. Guided by her inspiration she quickly took the ring off (it came quite easily this time), stuck it on to the carrot, and the latter disappeared, while the cry of sorrow ceased. But, oh, wonder of wonders! all at once Fräulein Aennchen was as pretty as ever, well-proportioned, and as fair and white as a country lady can be expected to be. She and her father rejoiced greatly, while Amandus stood puzzled, and not knowing what to make of it all.

Fräulein Aennchen took the spade from the maid, who had come running up, and flourished it in the air with a joyful shout of "Now let's set to work," in doing which she was unfortunate enough to deal Herr Amandus such a thwack on the head with it (just at the place where the Sensorium Commune is supposed to be situated) that he fell down as one dead.

Aennchen threw the murderous weapon far from her, cast herself down beside her beloved, and broke out into the most despairing lamentations, whilst the maid poured the contents of a watering pot over him, and Herr Dapsul quickly ascended the astronomic tower to consult the stars with as little delay as possible as to whether Herr Amandus was dead or not. But it was not long before the latter opened his eyes again, jumped to his legs, clasped Fräulein Aennchen in his arms, and cried, with all the rapture of affection, "Now, my best and dearest Anna, we are one another again."

The very remarkable, scarcely credible effect of this occurrence on the two lovers very soon made itself perceptible. Fräulein Aennchen took a dislike to touching a spade, and she did really reign like a queen over the vegetable world, inasmuch as, though taking care that her vassals were properly supervised and attended to, she set no hand to the work herself, but entrusted it to maids in whom she had confidence.

Herr Amandus, for his part, saw now that everything he had ever written in the shape of verses was wretched, miserable trash, and, burying himself in the works of the real poets, both of ancient and modern times, his being was soon so filled with a beneficent enthusiasm that no room was left for any consideration of himself. He arrived at the conviction that a real poem has got to be something other than a confused jumble of words shaken together under the influence of a crude, jejeune delirium, and threw all his own (so-called) poetry, of which he had had such a tremendous opinion, into the fire, becoming once more quite the sensible young gentleman, clear and open in heart and mind, which he had been originally.

And one morning Herr Dapsul did actually come down from his astronomical tower to go to church with Fräulein Aennchen and Herr Amandus von Nebelstern on the occasion of their marriage.

They led an exceedingly happy wedded life. But as to whether Herr Dapsul's union with the Sylphide Nehabilah ever actually came to anything the Chronicle of Dapsulheim is silent.

During the reading of this the Friends had laughed a good deal, and they were unanimously of opinion that, though there was not a great deal in the plot, yet that the details were so humorous and droll that, as a whole, the tale was a success.

"As to the plot," Vincenz said, "there is rather a curious circumstance connected with that. Not long since, happening to be dining at the table of a certain lady of princely rank, there was a lady present who had on a gold ring with a beautiful topaz, of which the remarkably antique-looking form and workmanship attracted universal attention. We thought it had been some precious heirloom, and were astonished to hear that it had been found sticking on a carrot dug up on her property a few years previously. Probably it had been lying pretty deep in the ground, and had been brought towards the surface when the land was trenched, so that the carrot had grown through it.

"The Princess pointed out what a good idea for a story

this suggested, and wished that I should set to work to write one at once on the subject. So, you see, I hadn't far to go for the idea of the 'Vegetable King and his People,' and I claim the invention of them for myself, for there isn't a trace of him to be found in Gabalis or any other book of the kind."

"Now," said Lothair, "I think we may say that on none of our former Serapion evenings has our fare been of a more various character than to-night. And it is good that we have managed to emerge from that gruesome darkness into which we had wandered somehow--I am sure it is hard to tell why--into the clear, brightsome light of day, although, no doubt, a serious, careful person might, with some reason, say that all the fantastic matter which we have so long been going on spinning and accumulating might have a considerable tendency to induce confusion of head, if not headache and feverishness."

"We should all do the best we can," said Theodore. "But let no one deem that his own particular qualities and powers constitute the norm of what the human understanding is to have laid before it. For there are people--good sensible folks enough in other respects--who are so easily made giddy in their heads that they think the rapid flight of an awakened imagination is the result of an unsound condition of mind. So that such people say, of this or the other writer, that he only writes when he is under the influence of intoxicating drinks, and attribute his imaginative writings to over-excited nerves, and a certain amount of deliriousness thence arising. But everybody knows that although a condition of mind raising from either of those causes can give rise to a happy thought, or fortunate idea, it is impossible that it can yield perfect and finished work, because that demands the very quietest study and consideration."

On this evening Theodore had set before his friends some remarkably superior wine sent to him by a friend on the Rhine. He poured what remained of it into the glasses, and said:--

"I cannot explain why it should be so; but a melancholy foreboding comes upon me that we are going to part for a long time, and may, perhaps, never meet again. But surely the remembrance of those Serapion evenings will long live in our minds. We have given free play to the capricious promptings of our fancy. Each of us has spoken out what he saw in his mind's eye, without supposing his ideas to be anything extraordinary, or giving them forth as being so, knowing well that the first essential of all effective composition is that kindly unpretendingness which is the thing that has the power to warm the heart and please the mind. If Fate is about to part us, then let us always faithfully follow the rule of Saint Serapion, and vowing this to each other, drink this last glass of our wine."

What Theodore suggested was accordingly done.